D0777394

LOCKDOWN

ATTACK ON EARTH

LOCKDOWN

RAELYN DRAKE

darbycreek

MINNEAPOLIS

Darby Creek
A division of Lerner Publishing Group, Inc.
241 First Avenue North
Minneapolis, MN 55401 USA

For reading levels and more information, look up this title at www.lernerbooks.com.

The images in this book are used with the permission of: WillJeffBarker/iStock/Getty Images; briddy_/iStock/Getty Images; ilobs/iStock/Getty Images; 4khz/DigitalVision Vectors/Getty Images.

Main body text set in Janson Text LT Std 12/17.5.
Typeface provided by Adobe Systems.

Library of Congress Cataloging-in-Publication Data

Names: Drake, Raelyn, author.
Title: Lockdown / Raelyn Drake.
Description: Minneapolis : Darby Creek, [2018] | Series: Attack on Earth | Summary: After a neighborhood watch-type community organization assumes control of their high school in the wake of an alien invasion, Sanjay and his two best friends begin to question whether they can trust the guards enforcing the lockdown.
Identifiers: LCCN 2017044213 (print) | LCCN 2017057790 (ebook) | ISBN 9781541525870 (eb pdf) | ISBN 9781541525764 (lb : alk. paper) | ISBN 9781541526303 (pb : alk. paper)
Subjects: | CYAC: Hostages—Fiction. | High schools—Fiction. | Schools—Fiction.
Classification: LCC PZ7.1.D74 (ebook) | LCC PZ7.1.D74 Lo 2018 (print) | DDC [Fic]—dc23

LC record available at https://lccn.loc.gov/2017044213

Manufactured in the United States of America
1-44560-35491-1/15/2018

TO MAX, FOR PESTERING ME UNTIL
I AGREED TO NAME A CHARACTER AFTER HIM.
HERE YA GO, BUDDY.

ON THE MORNING OF FRIDAY, OCTOBER 2, rings of light were seen coming down from the sky in several locations across the planet. By mid-morning, large spacecraft were visible through the clouds, hovering over major cities. The US government, along with others, attempted to make contact, without success.

At 9:48 that morning, the alien ships released an electromagnetic pulse, or EMP, around the world, disabling all electronics—including many vehicles and machines. All forms of communication technology were useless.

Now people could only wait and see what would happen with the "Visitors" next . . .

CHAPTER 1

Sanjay prodded his dead phone. Everything electronic had been fried when the EMP had hit that morning, and now his phone might as well be a shiny brick. He had never thought of himself as the type of person who was addicted to his phone, but now he couldn't think of a plan of action that *didn't* involve it. He couldn't call his parents, or check the news to find out what was going on, or even use the flashlight.

He and his friends, Chloe and Luis, were in Ms. Kim's physics class, and she had told them that this attack had all the hallmarks of a blast from an EMP. Sanjay had only ever seen stuff like that in science fiction movies—he felt like he was in one right now. They had all seen the giant air ships looming on the horizon like storm clouds. Right before the power grid went dark, the internet had been blowing up with pictures and videos from all over the world. People on social media rarely agreed on anything, but this time everyone seemed to come to the same conclusion: aliens were attacking Earth. And no one knew what these Visitors wanted.

But that had been almost an hour ago. Now they were cut off from the rest of the world. Ms. Kim insisted that school policy in any disaster or emergency situation was to keep students confined to the classroom. She wouldn't even let them leave to go to the bathroom until she could be sure the hallways were safe.

So everyone sat at their desks, shifting uncomfortably in the hard plastic seats and trying to come to terms with what was happening. Some students talked quietly with their friends. Others slept out of weariness and boredom, heads pillowed on arms folded across their desks. And some were crying, hands covering their faces, shoulders shaking occasionally with muffled sobs. Sanjay was grateful that, at the very least, he was stuck here with his two closest friends.

"For all we know," Chloe whispered, "we could be the last people on Earth."

"The blast just took out everything electric," Luis said. "It didn't vaporize everyone."

"That's my point," Chloe said. "We can't know that for sure because we can't contact anyone."

"Would you two cut it out?" Sanjay snapped. When class had started, he had been counting down the time to lunch. He'd even been looking forward to his afternoon study hour in the library. Mr. O'Donnell, the librarian, always had interesting stories that made the time pass quickly. Now it was lunchtime and there was no sign that things would magically go back to normal. Hunger and restlessness mixed with confusion and fear were not a recipe for a good mood.

Chloe and Luis stared at him. He was usually the most easygoing of the three of them. "Sorry, I just find it hard to care about the Visitors right now when my main concern is getting ahold of my mom."

"Quickly followed by a trip to the nearest bathroom," Luis muttered.

Chloe smirked. "Meanwhile, I'll be coming up with a plan to lead a rebellion against our alien overlords because *I* went to the bathroom before class," she said smugly.

There was a knock at the classroom door. "Ms. Kim? It's Officer Mendoza."

Ms. Kim hurried to unlock the door. Officer Alicia Mendoza, the school security cop, entered the room. Her hair was usually pulled back into a smooth bun, and she always had a smile ready for everyone, but today strands of hair had escaped her bun and her brow was creased with worry.

"Everyone okay in here?" she asked, scanning the students.

They all tried to ask their questions at once.

"What's going on, Officer Mendoza?" Sanjay asked.

"How are we going to contact our parents?" another student asked.

"What do the Visitors want?" Chloe shouted.

Officer Mendoza gave a small smile and held up her hands. The students quieted down. "I'm sorry, I wish I had more information for you. The fact is no one knows what's going on. We haven't received any sort of communication from outside the school yet. But I expect that emergency responders will be here soon to tell us what to do next. I really appreciate your cooperation in sitting tight while we try to figure this out. The primary goal of everyone in this school is keeping you safe, okay?"

"What about food?" one student asked.

"And bathrooms!" Luis asked.

"There's enough bottled water and canned food in the cafeteria kitchens to last us for a week or two," Officer Mendoza said.

"Do you really think we'll be here that long?" Sanjay asked.

"Hopefully not," Officer Mendoza said. She spoke quietly to Ms. Kim for a moment, then turned back to the students. "As for bathrooms, we think that it's safe enough at this point. But I want you to go in groups, and then I want you to return directly to this classroom so that it's easier to keep track of everyone. Listen to Ms. Kim."

Kids started to get up from their seats.

"Oh," Officer Mendoza added, "and I should probably mention that electricity is used to pump water into the school, so there's not going to be running water to flush the toilets."

Several students groaned loudly, but then they heard heavy, booted footsteps in the hallway.

"Did you release any other classes yet?" Ms. Kim whispered to Officer Mendoza

The officer's jaw clenched. "No."

"What if it's the Visitors?" one student hissed.

Officer Mendoza motioned for the students to be quiet. She crouched lower and peered around the doorframe, her hand reaching for the baton at her waist.

Sanjay and his friends couldn't see anything from where they were, but Ms. Kim must have been able to from where she was standing behind her desk. Her face suddenly showed a mix of confusion and relief. "Max Whitaker? What are you doing here?"

Sanjay exchanged surprised glances with Luis and Chloe. Max Whitaker had been a senior when they had started as freshmen. He had been one of the few upperclassmen who didn't mind hanging out with the younger kids. These days he worked at the coffee shop downtown that doubled as an art gallery. Sanjay, Chloe, and Luis liked to hang out there to do homework, and they enjoyed chatting with Max during his shifts.

But what is he doing here now? Sanjay wondered.

Max walked in, smiling at Ms. Kim. "Hey, everyone," he said. He looked as exhausted as Officer Mendoza, but he was still as effortlessly charming as always. Sanjay also noticed that Max was carrying a baseball bat.

Officer Mendoza looked at Ms. Kim and raised an eyebrow.

"He's a former student," Ms. Kim explained.

"I'm also a member of a community organization," Max added. "We're called the Citizens Active Protection Program, or CAPP for short. We're a neighborhood watch-style group committed to protecting this town in case of natural disasters and other emergencies. And I think we can all agree that this is an emergency."

Officer Mendoza shot a glance at the students. "Max, can I speak to you and Ms. Kim in the hallway for a moment?" Sanjay thought she sounded annoyed.

The adults stepped into the hallway and shut the classroom door behind them. Sanjay and his friends immediately crept closer to listen.

"This isn't normal protocol for an emergency response," they heard Officer Mendoza say.

"Well, this isn't a normal emergency," Max countered.

"Why haven't I heard anything about your group helping out?" she asked.

Max snorted. "The whole EMP thing has made it a little difficult to get communications out. But don't worry, all the right people know what's going on."

"I think it's all right, Alicia," Ms. Kim said to Officer Mendoza. "I remember Max, and he was always a good kid. Maybe we should listen to what he and his group have to say."

"It's not really *my* group," Max corrected. "It's the community's. I'm just like the . . . spokesman."

Sanjay didn't hear Officer Mendoza's response before Chloe dragged him and Luis back toward their desks. They clattered into their seats just as the door opened.

"CAPP is here to look after you guys," Max said, continuing his speech to the class as though he hadn't been interrupted, "just like Officer Mendoza and your teachers. Before the EMPs shut down communications, local law enforcement had begun evacuating the rest of the town to an emergency shelter."

"So are we going there too?" Sanjay asked.

"We'd love to be able to have you all go there so you can find your families, but it's very dangerous outside right now. CAPP's job is to keep an eye on you all until it's safe to move you to the emergency shelter."

"I don't care if it's safe or not," Luis said. "I'd rather be in danger and with my family than safe but stuck at school."

"Look, man, I know you'd do anything for your family," Max said. "I would too. I love this community, and I'm not going to let some stupid aliens take that away from me. But imagine what your parents would say if they found out that I knew the dangers and didn't keep you safe."

"Yeah, I guess," Luis grumbled. "So, what are we supposed to do then?"

"CAPP has brought extra supplies. We have more than enough food, plus blankets so we can set up makeshift beds in the library and gym. We even brought enough jugs of water, so you guys can use the bucket method to flush the toilets and still have enough drinking water."

Luis sighed in relief, but Chloe frowned. "Hey, Max, what's the bat for?"

Max smiled grimly. "It's for protection."

CHAPTER 2

The rest of the day was spent getting the gym and library set up as makeshift sleeping spaces. Sanjay and his friends were in the group of two hundred or so students assigned to the library. It was weird seeing half of his school crammed in together. The tables were pushed to the edges of the room so that pillows, blankets, and sleeping bags could be lined up across the floor and in between bookshelves. The sun set quickly this time of year, and by the time they had finished, the school had grown dark.

The full moon cast a little light in through the library's windows, but Sanjay was still thankful for the packs of candles that CAPP had brought with them. He sat on his sleeping bag with Chloe and Luis on either side of him. The other students sat in similar clusters around the room, loudly and anxiously discussing the day's events. Sanjay heard the words "the Visitors" repeated again and again. He could just imagine what the librarian would have to say about the noise level of the conversations.

Sanjay peered around the dim library. "I wonder where Mr. O'Donnell is. I would've thought he'd want to be here with us in the library."

"Come to think of it, where are *any* of the teachers?" Chloe asked, narrowing her eyes. "I haven't even seen Ms. Kim since they let us out of the classrooms."

Sanjay walked over to a CAPPer who was standing nearby. *Because apparently high schoolers need a babysitter to get ready for bed*, he thought. He recognized the woman from the bike shop downtown. She had a stun gun hooked on her belt and she wasn't smiling, but then again not many people were feeling cheerful right now.

"Excuse me?" he said to the woman. "Ma'am?"

She looked at him like he was wasting her time. "Yeah?"

Sanjay tried to keep his tone polite in spite of her gruff response. "My friends and I were just wondering when we would be able to leave the school."

"You can't," she said.

"We have to leave the school at some point if we want to find our parents."

"The school is on lockdown," she said. "No one comes in, and no one leaves."

Sanjay frowned. "But—"

"It's not safe," the woman snapped and walked off to talk to another CAPPer by the library's checkout desk.

Sanjay joined Chloe and Luis back by their sleeping spaces. The puzzled frowns on their faces made it clear that they had heard the odd exchange. But before Sanjay could discuss it with them, Max came over carrying a large cardboard box filled with blankets. "Don't mind Paula," he said in a stage whisper. "She's like that to everyone."

He handed them each a blanket. "With no electricity to run the heat, the school is only going to get colder."

Chloe elbowed Sanjay and gave him a look. "Uh, Max," Sanjay asked. "Where are all the teachers?"

Max laughed. "That's sweet that you're worried about your teachers. They're all in the teachers' lounge since there wasn't enough room for them to sleep in the library or gym. CAPP has also set up a base in the main office."

Sanjay knew where that was. There was a set of glass doors near the front entrance of the school that led to a suite of offices for the principal, secretary, and guidance counselor. The teachers' lounge was in there too.

"Could we talk to Mr. O'Donnell?"

Max looked confused. "The librarian?"

"Yeah," Sanjay said. "I was hoping he might have some idea of how to communicate with the emergency shelter. He told me he used to be part of the National Guard when he was younger."

"Oh yeah," Max said. "I forgot about that . . ." He stared off into space, as if lost in thought.

"Great idea, Sanjay," Chloe said excitedly. "I bet he would know all sorts of survival skills and how to deal with emergency situations."

Max smiled. "I like where your head's at, Chloe. I'll make sure to ask him." He handed them granola bars and bottled water. "Sorry dinner isn't very exciting, but we're still taking stock of the canned food in the cafeteria."

Chloe snorted as she unwrapped her granola bar. "Earth was just attacked by aliens. We're not expecting fine dining."

"We *are* expecting some answers, though," Sanjay said. "Like when we'll be able to try to contact our parents."

Max lowered his voice so only Sanjay, Luis, and Chloe could hear him. "I wish I had answers for you, but nothing is certain right now. To be honest, we're just as scared as you guys. Same with the teachers. But I promise we'll get through this crisis together, okay? You all just have to trust us. We're doing what's best for this community."

Sanjay nodded. "Thanks for looking out for us, Max."

Max smiled at the three of them. "Of course. What are friends for?"

He went off to distribute blankets and food to the next group of kids, clustered together in another corner of the library.

Officer Mendoza approached, almost as if she had been waiting for Max to leave. "How are you holding up?" she asked quietly, her eyes still crinkled with worry.

Sanjay shrugged. "Hanging in there."

Officer Mendoza smiled weakly. "You kids are tough. Some of the other students won't stop complaining about the lack of computers and running water."

"I'm more worried about what CAPP is doing here," Chloe muttered.

Sanjay frowned at her. "You heard Max," he said. "CAPP is here to protect the school and keep us safe."

Chloe sighed. "Max is nice and all, but that doesn't mean I trust CAPP just because he says I should." She turned to Officer Mendoza. "Do *you* think we can trust CAPP?"

Officer Mendoza waited a beat too long

before answering. "I'm sure it's all right—"

"Oh, c'mon, Officer Mendoza," Chloe said. "It's starting to seem like no one respects us enough to tell us the truth."

The officer rubbed her temples. "I don't want you kids to worry about it . . . but I do agree with Chloe," she admitted in a whisper. "I've never heard of CAPP. I recognize a lot of the people from around town, but just because a bunch of citizens armed themselves with stun guns and baseball bats doesn't mean they're qualified to guard students during an alien attack."

Sanjay turned to Luis. "What do you think?"

Luis shrugged. "Max seems to be the only one who wants to talk to us. All the other CAPPers just glare at us."

"Everyone is stressed right now," Sanjay pointed out.

"Then why wouldn't Max let us go talk to Mr. O'Donnell ourselves?" Chloe asked.

Sanjay couldn't think of an answer to that one. Max hadn't specifically said they *couldn't* talk to the librarian, but he had changed the subject and seemed to avoid answering their questions. Sanjay tried to ignore the twisting feeling in the pit of his stomach. *Everyone's just imagining things*, he told himself.

"Either way," Officer Mendoza said, "I'm going to stop by the main office and talk to these CAPPers. See if I can get some straightforward answers on what's going on and what the plan is. If there even is a plan."

She turned to leave, then stopped and said, "Look, if I'm not back by tomorrow morning . . ."

She trailed off and shook her head, as if she'd thought better of what she was going to say.

"Just promise me you'll look after yourselves. And be careful who you trust."

* * *

Sanjay curled up on his side in the dark library, trying to ignore the rustling and hushed conversations of the other students. He never would've thought he would be sleeping in the library with half his classmates. Luis snored nearby. The library's carpet was thin and slightly musty, but it was better than the hardwood floor in the gym. Sanjay pulled the blanket tighter around him. It was only October, but the outside temperature at night was hovering just above freezing, and the school wasn't much warmer. The CAPPers had let the students get their jackets and hats and scarves from their lockers, but most of that gear was more suited for fashion than warmth.

"I still can't believe this is all really happening," Sanjay whispered to Chloe, who lay next to him.

Chloe sighed. "Whenever I'd watch a sci-fi movie where aliens attack Earth, I used to plan out what I would do in that situation. The problem is, all of my plans involved tech and gadgets and other things that run on electricity. We don't have phones or running water or computers or even cars. How are we supposed to fight back against enemies in spaceships when we're stuck in the Dark Ages?"

"Guess that's up to you to figure out, if you're so keen to lead the resistance."

Chloe flailed out with her arm in the dark trying to smack Sanjay playfully. He snickered, trying to dodge by rolling out of the way.

"Shut up and go to sleep!" a CAPPer grumbled at them, jolting Sanjay back to the harsh reality of their current situation. This wasn't a sleepover or some school camping trip—they were stuck in lockdown at their school and cut off from their families.

The library grew still again.

Several minutes went by, and Sanjay assumed that Chloe had fallen asleep.

But then: "Sanjay," she whispered again, so quietly he could barely hear her this time.

"Yeah?"

"Do you think everyone . . . do you think my aunt and uncle survived the attack?"

Her voice shook slightly, and Sanjay thought she might be crying. He felt like crying himself when he thought about his mom and what might be happening outside the school.

"I'm sure they're okay," Sanjay said. "I'm sure everyone made it to the emergency shelter just fine."

"Yeah, you're probably right," Chloe said softly, clearing her throat. "Thanks."

She sounded comforted. Sanjay hoped he had managed to convince her that everything would be all right.

Now if only he could convince himself.

CHAPTER 3

Sanjay was awoken by the light streaming
in through the library's windows and the
movements of his classmates.

Memories of the attack and worries about
his mom came flooding back, destroying
the last remnants of his peaceful dreams.
But beyond the stress, he just felt physically
terrible. He was cold and his muscles were stiff
from sleeping on the uncomfortable floor. And
he didn't even need to test his breath to know it
was awful.

He got up, folded his blanket, and sorted
through his belongings from his backpack
and locker. It wasn't much. His phone and
headphones and the school-assigned tablet

were all useless. He doubted his geometry
and English textbooks were going to be very
handy in the current situation. That just left
pens and paper, half a bottle of orange juice,
his wallet and keys, a few sticks of gum, and
some paper clips.

He felt something in the bottom of his
backpack and pulled out a travel-sized tube
of toothpaste. He must have left it in there
after his family's vacation a couple of weeks
ago. There was no toothbrush, though. He
squeezed a tiny bit of toothpaste on his finger
and rubbed it over his teeth and gums. He
took a sip of water and swished it around in his
mouth. At least he could face the current crisis
with minty-fresh breath.

Chloe woke up soon after, squinting
sleepily. She tugged a hand through her hair
and sighed heavily. "Not a dream, then?"

"Nope," Sanjay said, passing her the
toothpaste.

They shook Luis awake. He mumbled a
protest and tried to turn over to go back to
sleep, but then he quickly sat up, scanning the

room anxiously. "Is Officer Mendoza back yet?"

Sanjay shook his head, when a voice behind them made them all jump.

"She won't be back for a while," Max said. "But I come bearing breakfast!"

He held up a couple of boxes of toaster pastries and several of jars of peanut butter. The other students started to line up enthusiastically.

Sanjay leaned in close and spoke softly to Max so that only Chloe and Luis could hear their conversation. "Are you sure Officer Mendoza is all right?" he asked.

Max met Sanjay's eyes, and for a split second, Sanjay could have sworn he saw something there. Annoyance? Fear? But then it was replaced with Max's signature charming smile. "Of course she's fine. She can handle herself." He shifted away from them and started handing out toaster pastries to the other students.

"Where'd she go?" Sanjay pressed.

"Huh?" Max said, as though he had already moved on from the conversation. He shrugged.

"Oh, uh, I don't know where exactly, but somewhere outside the school. She said she wanted to check the area for anyone who might need help, see if she could find some extra supplies, stuff like that." He handed breakfast to Sanjay and his friends.

Sanjay thought of the expression in Officer Mendoza's eyes when she told them to be careful who they trusted. *But she didn't mean Max . . .*

Did she?

As if he could read Sanjay's thoughts, Max smiled. "C'mon, Sanjay. You know I've got your back. You can trust me."

Sanjay forced himself to match Max's smile. "Of course. Thanks, man."

He didn't let the smile drop until Max had turned his attention back to the line of students still waiting to receive their breakfast.

Sanjay, Chloe, and Luis waited to talk until they were back by their makeshift beds.

"See?" Chloe hissed once she was sure Max couldn't hear her. "I know you don't want to believe it because Max has always seemed like such a cool guy, but you have to admit that something is seriously weird here."

Sanjay nodded reluctantly. "You're right, something's off."

Luis rolled his eyes. "Max is totally hiding something from us."

"Maybe the other members of CAPP just won't let him tell us everything," Sanjay pointed out, even though he knew he was grasping at straws.

Chloe sneaked a glance at the other CAPPers in the library. Two stood near the doors. Another three CAPPers were helping Max hand out breakfast, taking attendance of all the students, and listening to students' requests. Sanjay couldn't help feeling that the CAPPers near the door looked more like bouncers than bodyguards.

Chloe motioned for Sanjay and Luis to come with her. "Follow my lead," she whispered to them, before approaching the CAPPers near the library doors.

"Good morning," she said brightly. "My friends and I were wondering if we could go eat our breakfast in the courtyard. It may be the end of the world, but at least it's a sunny fall morning, right?"

"It's not safe," grumbled one of the CAPPers.

Chloe smiled and spread her hands out. "Oh, c'mon, we'll just be in the courtyard. It's completely surrounded by the school—there aren't any doors leading out of the building. We could use a little sunlight and fresh air."

When the CAPPers didn't answer, Chloe tried another approach. She lowered her voice and said, "Okay, look, I'm not trying to make a big deal out of this, but I have trouble with enclosed spaces. I'm sort of freaking out a little." She pressed a hand to her chest as if to steady her breathing and inhaled slowly. Her breath sounded ragged. "I'm starting to feel really woozy, and I think some fresh air would help me calm down."

The CAPPer took a step forward and put his hand to his waist, letting it rest on his stun gun. "We can't have individuals threaten the safety of this community. If you refuse to follow instructions, we'll need to do what it takes to keep everything under control."

Chloe looked like she wanted to call their bluff, and Sanjay easily pictured her trying to rush past the men. But he wasn't ready to test whether those stun guns were just for show. He grabbed her by the elbow and shot her a warning look.

Chloe sighed and stepped back, following Sanjay and Luis back toward the other students.

Once they were out of earshot, Luis muttered, "Keep every*thing* under control? Or every*one*?"

"I can't believe they would prioritize their stupid lockdown over a potential health emergency," Chloe said.

"Yeah, but you aren't actually feeling claustrophobic," Sanjay said.

She waved a hand. "Well, I wanted to see if *something* would get us out of the school. And it doesn't matter if I was making it up or not—a student told them she had a health concern and they didn't do anything about it."

"So what do we do now?" Luis asked. "By my count, there have to be at least thirty CAPPers in the building."

"That's not so bad," said Chloe. "The students outnumber them by a lot."

"Yeah, but none of us have stun guns."

Sanjay realized that Luis and Chloe were acting as if it was up to *them* to get to the bottom of this. Part of him wanted to tell them to chill out. After all, there were plenty of adults around. Why should the three of them feel responsible for the fate of the whole school?

Then again, maybe they had a point. Even a day ago, Sanjay had been willing to let Max be the person who called the shots. But now Sanjay wasn't sure he could be trusted.

"We need to go talk to the teachers," Sanjay said. "Mr. O'Donnell might know some emergency survival skills, and Ms. Kim might have more information on the EMP aftereffects."

"But the teachers' lounge is in the main office," Luis pointed out. "And we can't even get out of the library."

Sanjay thought back to everything he'd learned about the library during study hall. "I have an idea about that," he whispered. "Tonight, after lights-out, let's meet in the back of the library by Mr. O'Donnell's office. If I'm right, then there's another way out of the library than the main door. And if I'm wrong, or if we get caught, the CAPPers can't get mad at us because we will still be in the library, just like they told us."

"C'mon," Luis said, nodding, "let's go sit with the others. We should probably stop slinking around and whispering all day or the CAPPers will get suspicious. We don't want Max to think we're plotting something."

Chloe gave her best innocent look. "Who, *us*? Where would he *ever* get that idea?" She winked at them and went off to join the other girls from the volleyball team.

CHAPTER 4

The rest of the day seemed to drag on
painfully slowly for Sanjay. Every so often
someone burst into tears or started to panic
about whether their families were safe. But for
the most part, the students kept calm. They
complained about the bathrooms and the
food and how their phones were now useless,
and they speculated wildly about the reasons
why the Visitors would choose to attack Earth
at this particular time. They occasionally
threw glances over their shoulders at the
armed CAPPers, and they spoke in hushed
voices. But if his classmates were hatching
secret plans of their own, they didn't let
Sanjay and his friends know. Although he

certainly didn't tell them anything about his own plan either. The fewer people who were in on tonight's wplan, the better chance it had of succeeding.

After an uninspiring dinner of more granola bars, bottled water, and cold canned baked beans, the students once again set up their makeshift blanket beds. They grumbled about how cold and uncomfortable the sleeping arrangements were until the CAPPers got frustrated and shouted at everyone to shut up.

Sanjay lay there with his eyes closed until the CAPPers blew out the candles placed throughout the library. He wondered where Max had gone. Without him there, the CAPPers seemed less concerned with being polite. Sanjay figured that they weren't necessarily bad people, but they were terrified, stressed, and trying to keep some semblance of order. Unlike the teachers, they didn't have years of experience with getting a bunch of high schoolers to behave.

He wondered if Max really was lying to them or hiding something from them. Sanjay desperately wanted to hold on to the hope that Max wasn't the bad guy in all this.

The room was now silent and almost completely dark, except for a dim puddle of light seeping under the doors. Two CAPPers were posted right outside with some candles placed in the hallway to help them see. But no CAPPers had stayed in the library itself, and Sanjay felt confident he and his friends would be able to sneak around without detection. As long as none of their fellow students noticed them and gave them away.

A chorus of gentle, measured breathing came from the sleeping students. It was time to put the plan into action.

Mr. O'Donnell's office was at the back of the library, behind a door marked STAFF ONLY. Sanjay had paid enough attention during study hall to notice that the office doubled as a storage room, and that the door was often left unlocked.

Sanjay rolled over onto his feet in a low crouch and looked around, hoping he wouldn't step on someone's hand or bang his shins on

one of the metal bookshelves. He didn't hear
Chloe or Luis moving yet, but he couldn't
tell if that was because they were staying
absolutely silent or if they had already moved
to the meeting place . . . or if they had fallen
asleep waiting.

It was so dark, and even once Sanjay's eyes
had adjusted, he still could barely see. He had
never noticed before how much he took things
like streetlights for granted. Even when he
went camping with his mom, there were still
electric lights illuminating the area around the
bathrooms. He again wished he could use the
flashlight on his phone.

Halfway across the library, Sanjay suddenly
noticed that the CAPPers' light from the
hallway was growing brighter. He dove behind
the checkout desk, heart racing. His back was
to the hallway, but he heard the soft *swish* of
the doors brushing over the carpet as they
swung open. The CAPPers lifted their lights
up high, casting shadows on the back wall of
the library.

A moment passed in silence, and then

Sanjay heard the doors click shut again. He waited a full minute, counting the seconds in his head, to make sure the coast was clear before he left his hiding spot. He continued his crawl to the back corner of the library. At one point, he nearly tripped over a sleeping student and barely caught himself on a bookshelf before he fell on top of them. *This plan had better work*, he thought.

He saw something move in the darkness next to him and felt his heart skip a beat. A moment later he realized it was Chloe, crouching down behind a table near the door to Mr. O'Donnell's office. She held a finger to her lips. He could just barely make out the details of her face in the dark. He sighed with relief when he realized Luis was there too. *So far, so good*, he thought.

Sanjay opened the door as quietly as he could. Luis kept his attention focused in the direction of the door to the library, keeping alert for any sign of movement that might indicate that the CAPPers were coming back in for another check.

The door swung open smoothly and soundlessly. They paused again, listening, but all was still. Sanjay allowed himself to breathe a quiet sigh of relief. If this had been his own house, the door hinges would have squeaked loud enough to alert the aliens up in their spaceships.

He felt a pang when he thought about his house and wondered if his mom had made it safely to the emergency shelter. Then he realized that they had only heard about this emergency shelter from Max. If the CAPPers were hiding information from the students, they could have hidden the truth about their families as well. Maybe the CAPPers didn't actually know whether anyone else was safe. He shoved the panicky feeling to the back of his mind. He *had* to believe that his mother was all right. He didn't have time to worry. He would have to stay strong.

As he stared into the dark room, Sanjay realized the flaw in his plan. As dark as the library was, at least there was still a little moonlight and the candlelight from the hallway. Mr. O'Donnell's office was windowless. Sanjay fought the instinct to feel blindly along the wall for a light switch. It wouldn't do them any good now.

He knew that the room existed, and he knew that there was a second door that led out to the hallway because he had seen Mr. O'Donnell use it. But Sanjay didn't know the layout of the room well enough to rely on feeling his way around. He was bound to knock something over.

Luis suddenly shoved Sanjay and Chloe from behind, pushing them into the office. "Quick!" he hissed. He pulled the door shut behind them, pitching them into complete blackness.

"CAPPers," he whispered in explanation, though Sanjay had already guessed that.

In the darkness, Sanjay sensed someone edge past him. "Chloe, what are you doing?"

"We can't just stand there and wait to get caught. Help me search for the back door, or anything else useful."

Sanjay felt the corner of a desk next to

him and edged along it, patting the surface carefully. He could hear the others feeling around too. Then Chloe gasped, and they heard a strange whirring sound. Sanjay couldn't make out what it was, but he hoped that the door was thick enough to block most of the sound.

"Check out what I just found," Chloe said.

Suddenly a flashlight turned on. Chloe grinned at them as Sanjay and Luis blinked in the unexpected light.

"What is that?" Sanjay asked.

"It's a hand-crank flashlight," she quietly explained. "Looks pretty old. It doesn't run on batteries—you just have to crank this handle a bunch to power it. It's kinda loud, but then it gives you about a half hour of light. My uncle keeps one just like this in the basement for emergencies."

She shone the flashlight beam around the room. Besides Mr. O'Donnell's desk, the room was filled with piles of books to shelve, boxes, and other odds and ends.

"Hey," Luis said from where he was

digging through a set of drawers. "I found a screwdriver." He held it up excitedly.

"Really?" Chloe asked sarcastically.

He glared at her. "Whatever. It might be good for self-defense in a pinch." He tucked the screwdriver into one of his boots.

Chloe nodded and continued directing the flashlight beam along the walls. "I'm not seeing another door," she said.

Sanjay's heart sank as he looked around the room. "No," he said, refusing to believe what his eyes were telling him. "No, there *has* to be a second door. I swear I've seen Mr. O'Donnell come out of it into the hallway." Had he really put his friends through all of this for nothing?

Chloe frowned, but Luis grabbed his arm. "There!"

Sanjay stared at the stretch of wall where Luis was pointing. At first he only saw a tall filing cabinet, but then he noticed what was peeking out from behind it. The door was mostly blocked by the cabinet, but it was there.

"Ugh, how are we going to move that thing

without making a huge racket?" Chloe asked.

"What's it doing in front of the door in the first place?" demanded Luis, as if the cabinet had personally insulted them.

"It looks super heavy," Chloe said. "I'm not even sure we could get it to budge without one of those dolly things movers use."

Sanjay walked over to examine the filing cabinet. He turned to Chloe and Luis and grinned. "Check this out."

He grabbed the sides of the filing cabinet and pulled. Instead of screeching and sliding on the cement floor, the whole thing rolled smoothly toward him. The door was hidden but still easily accessible.

Chloe's mouth fell open. "He put the filing cabinet on wheels?"

"Now's not the time to question things!" Luis hissed, pushing the cabinet further out of the way. "I don't care if this thing has rocket boosters as long as we can move it."

Sanjay paused with his hand on the doorknob. "Chloe, turn off the flashlight," he whispered. "If there are CAPPers outside the door in this section of the hallway, they would definitely notice the light."

They were plunged into darkness once more. After giving their eyes a moment to adjust, Sanjay turned the door handle. The door opened inward, and he stared out the narrow crack into the hallway. "Looks like the coast is clear," he whispered. He couldn't see any light from wandering guards. They just had to hope that the CAPPers hadn't decided to sneak around in the dark like *they* currently were.

"What next?" Chloe asked.

"We head for the main office," Sanjay explained. "If we can get there without being seen by any CAPPers, then maybe we can get to the teachers' lounge and find out if the teachers know what's going on."

"What happens if they catch us?" Luis asked quietly.

Sanjay had been trying to avoid thinking of that part. "Worst case scenario, they march us back to the library and yell at us a bit, right?" he asked.

"I don't know," Chloe said, "they do have stun guns and baseball bats and . . . who knows what else."

"But they wouldn't use those on us, would they?" Sanjay asked. "I mean, the threat was probably just a bluff to try to scare us into good behavior. They wouldn't *actually* hurt a bunch of high schoolers . . . right?" Even as he said it, the words sounded hollow to him. Maybe it was all just wishful thinking.

Chloe frowned. "Aliens just attacked Earth. I'm beginning to think that anything is possible."

Sanjay swallowed the lump in his throat. "Just don't get caught."

CHAPTER 5

The three of them crept quietly into the deserted hallway. If they took the most direct route to the main office, that would bring them past the library and the CAPPers who stood guard. So instead, their plan was to take the stairs to the second floor, which they figured would be less carefully guarded than the floor with all the students.

With any luck, they could make their way to the front of the building and come back down the set of stairs in that corner of the building. It would put them in the hallway just past the main office.

Sanjay was hoping that the CAPPers would be expecting any students or other unwanted guests to come from the direction of the library. Mainly, the plan relied on the CAPPers knowing less about the layout of the school then they did. Max, and probably a few others, had been students here once too, but that had been years ago.

Although they knew the school well, it was still strange to be sneaking around it at night. The dark and shadowy hallways looked odd to them, and it took them a minute to get their bearings. It was hard to believe that just a couple of days ago, these hallways had been filled with students talking, rushing around, and using their phones. Now even their muffled footfalls seemed to echo off the metal lockers. Sanjay had never realized how much background noise was created by the hum of electric lights and generators.

They were halfway up the stairs when they heard voices coming from above. They froze, then ran back down the way they'd come. It was nearly impossible to get down the stairs quickly without making too much noise. They made it to the bottom with just seconds to spare. Thinking quickly, Sanjay backed into the space under the stairs, pulling Chloe and Luis in behind him.

The stairs above them echoed with the heavy footsteps of the CAPPers. They chatted openly, although their banter sounded strained with nervousness. But that was what everyone sounded like since the attack. Sanjay wondered if people would ever feel safe and relaxed again.

"I don't see why we've got to patrol the hallways," said the first CAPPer.

"The kids might try something," the second CAPPer replied.

The first CAPPer snorted. "I'm more worried about the aliens than a bunch of teens. And besides, without their smartphones they're lost."

The second CAPPer chuckled. "No more than the rest of us."

As the CAPPers reached the bottom of the stairs, Sanjay tried to slow his panicked breathing into steady, soundless breaths.

"You going to guard the library?" the first CAPPer asked.

"Nah," the second CAPPer replied. "I'm on basement duty tonight."

Their voices faded as they moved away. Sanjay, Chloe, and Luis all heaved a sigh of relief.

"What's 'basement duty'?" Chloe asked in a hushed voice.

Luis shrugged. "Beats me."

Sanjay shook his head. "Add it to the list of things we still need to figure out."

Chloe looked up the dark stairwell. "So I guess the second floor is guarded after all."

"We'll have to risk it," Sanjay said. "There *might* be more guards up there, but we know for sure that there are CAPPers guarding the hallway down here."

They crept up the stairs again. They paused when they got to the landing, peering around the corner and listening for footsteps or voices. When they heard nothing, they continued up. They practically crawled the last couple of steps, trying to get a view of what awaited them in the upstairs hallway before they went rushing in unawares.

Nothing moved, so the three of them crept out of the stairwell, keeping low and hugging the wall as they went. The hallway was deserted, but candlelight spilled out of one of the classrooms closest to the staircase they needed, the one that would lead them to the main office. They could hear several voices. Clearly the CAPPers stationed up here were less on their guard than the ones in the downstairs hallway, but that didn't mean they would let three students wander the hallways at night. They would still raise the alarm, and Sanjay didn't want to find out what that would involve.

But if they were going to reach the staircase at the other end of the hallway, they would have to sneak right past the open door.

"There's no way we'll get by without them noticing us," Luis whispered.

"What if we create some sort of distraction?" Sanjay suggested.

"How would we do that?" Luis asked.

Sanjay ran through a list of options in his head. But all of them seemed to require one of them getting caught. And even then, they still relied on the CAPPers settling for the one student left as bait instead of chasing the other two.

"We could just crawl by on our stomachs, army-style," Sanjay said.

Chloe shook her head and sighed. "Even if we stayed in the shadows on the opposite side of the hallway, they would still see us the instant they looked up."

Sanjay cupped his hands and blew on them to warm up his cold fingers while they debated. He could hear the wind howling around the building outside. "I think I have an idea," he said.

The hallway had a large window to let in natural light. With a glance down the hall to the classroom where the CAPPers were, Sanjay stood up to examine the window. Obviously it didn't open far enough for someone to crawl out of, but if you pushed on the bottom of the pane, it would swing outward a couple of inches. Sanjay unlatched it and pushed carefully until the window was open. The chill wind whistled in through the crack.

"What good does that do?" Luis asked. "It's cold enough in here as it is."

He explained the rest of his plan to his friends.

Holding their shoes, they crept down the hallway in their socks, edging toward the occupied classroom. If they could slam the door shut, they could run past the classroom in the couple of seconds it would take for the CAPPers to wonder what had happened. Sanjay thought they could just about make it to the stairwell at that end of the hallway. Hopefully, the CAPPers would notice the open window and think the wind had blown the door shut.

They stood in a line, backs pressed up against the wall, with Sanjay closest to the door. Sanjay took a deep, shaky breath and pushed the door. The door was heavier than he had counted on, and he nearly lost his balance as it swung shut with a slam that echoed down the hallway.

Luis and Chloe sprinted past him. Sanjay heard the confused voices of the CAPPers inside the room as he started running. Hoping his socks wouldn't slip on the smooth floor tiles, Sanjay pounded down the hall.

Chloe and Luis reached the stairwell first, racing down the steps. Sanjay could hear the door handle begin to turn and practically threw himself down the stairwell. The momentum sent him tumbling into Chloe and Luis at the bottom, but they managed to catch themselves. The classroom door flew open, and they froze. Sanjay leaned on the handrail for support as he struggled to catch his breath.

Stay quiet, he told himself firmly.

"Hmm, looks like it was nothing," one of the CAPPers was saying.

"Are you sure?" another CAPPer asked.

"Yeah, look!" the first CAPPer said then. "Some idiot left the window at the end of the hallway open."

He grumbled as he stomped down the hallway in the opposite direction. They heard him shut the window and walk back to the classroom, still muttering.

Sanjay whispered a silent thank you when he heard the CAPPer close the door behind him this time. If they had to escape back the way they had come, they had a much better chance if that door was closed. The same trick would never work again.

Luis gave him an air high five.

Sanjay smiled weakly and got to his feet. His legs felt like jelly, but he and his friends were only halfway to their destination. And they didn't know any more about the CAPPers or their plans than they had when they had left the library. They couldn't give up now.

CHAPTER 6

With their shoes back on, the three of them
crept quietly down the stairwell, pausing every
so often to listen for footsteps or voices. But
everything was silent.

Almost eerily silent, Sanjay thought as they
peered around the corner at the bottom of
the stairs. If the teachers and the rest of the
CAPPers were stationed in the main office
like Max had said, then why was it so quiet?
Even if most people were asleep, someone
would be standing guard, just like at the
library. And the shifting and breathing and
snoring of a bunch of people ought to create
some noise. The entire hallway looked and felt
abandoned.

They crept down the hallway to the main office door. If anyone happened to turn the corner, he or she would see the three of them instantly. There were no classrooms to duck into, just some locked janitorial and maintenance closets. Sanjay felt horribly exposed, like a prey animal sneaking into a predator's den.

"What do we do if the main office is full of CAPPers?" Luis asked.

Chloe sighed. "Shout for help and hope the teachers take our side," she said. "I'm only half joking."

"Yeah," Sanjay agreed. "There's not really any way for us to sneak in. There's only the one door."

They reached the glass panels on either side of the door. The main office was dark, lit only by the moonlight through an outside window. They couldn't see any candlelight inside.

Sanjay cautiously tried the doorknob. It was unlocked, and the door swung open soundlessly. He looked at Chloe and Luis, but they shrugged, so Sanjay eased inside the door, followed closely by his friends. They closed the door carefully behind them.

They didn't dare use the hand-crank flashlight until they were absolutely certain that there were no CAPPers here. The main office had a secretary's desk and a small waiting area with a coffee table and a couch. Directly to the left was the door to the school nurse's office. The right wall was lined with doors that led to the offices of the principal, vice principal, and school guidance counselor. And in the back left corner, behind the secretary's desk, was a door marked **TEACHERS' LOUNGE**.

The floor in the office suite was covered with the same thin institutional carpet as the library, and they padded around noiselessly. They peered behind the secretary's desk and listened at the closed doors of the offices, but they didn't see any sleeping figures or hear any sounds. Chloe motioned that they should open the office doors and check inside, but Sanjay shook his head. If any CAPPers were sleeping in those rooms, there was a chance they wouldn't hear three intruders enter the Teachers' Lounge. But the sound of a door opening could easily wake them.

The three of them made their way back to the teachers' lounge and opened the door.

Sanjay wasn't sure what he had expected to find.

The best-case scenario he had imagined was finding all the teachers, including Mr. O'Donnell, Ms. Kim, and Officer Mendoza, so that they could all discuss what was going on at the school.

The worst-case scenario was that they would walk into a room of CAPPers who were armed to the teeth and angry.

Okay, the *real* worst-case scenario would be finding the room full of aliens. But he was trying to be realistic here.

But he hadn't expected it to be empty.

After a moment, Chloe gave the flashlight a few cranks and shone it around the room. Not only was it empty, but it looked like it had been ransacked. Cupboard doors stood open, and the supplies for making coffee had been spilled on the ground. It looked like the instant coffee and creamer tubs had been taken, leaving only a few wooden stir sticks and coffee filters.

"Where is everyone?" Luis asked. "If the teachers aren't here, then where are they?"

"Max must have lied to us," Sanjay said. His mouth felt dry. "Either the teachers left the school and abandoned us here or . . ." He couldn't bring himself to finish the thought, but he could see from the expression in Chloe and Luis's eyes that they were thinking the same thing.

Chloe opened a closet next to the now-powerless fridge. "This supply closet is empty," she reported, panning her flashlight over the shelves. "Or at least all the useful stuff is gone. There's some office supplies and stationery, but there are a lot of empty spots on the shelves that are labeled for things like paper towels, tissues, first aid kits . . . Do you think the teachers took those with them?"

Luis shook his head. "My bet is definitely on the CAPPers coming down here and ransacking the place. I sure hope they meant to share the supplies with the students."

"We've got to find the teachers," Sanjay said. "It's not just about asking them what to do either—I'm honestly worried about them."

"Well," said Chloe, "since they're not here, I'm guessing they're in the basement."

Sanjay remembered the CAPPers upstairs talking about basement duty. "Good thinking!"

"Hold on, though," said Luis. "If the teachers are being held there against their will that means the basement is probably heavily guarded. We can't go up against a bunch of CAPPers on our own."

"I agree," Chloe said, folding her arms. "I think we need to get help from the outside."

Sanjay blinked at her. "Outside? You mean leave the school?"

Chloe rolled her eyes. "I can see that the Stockholm syndrome is already setting in. Yes, Sanjay, we should leave the school! Once we find our parents we can come back here and make sure the teachers are safe."

"Agreed," said Luis. "I vote that we bust out of here and try to find our parents."

"We don't know what sort of dangers are out there," Sanjay protested. "We can't prepare if we don't know what we'll face."

"The CAPPers lied about the teachers," Chloe pointed out. "Maybe they lied about what's going on out there too."

"They didn't lie about the alien attack," Sanjay snapped.

Chloe fell silent and dropped her arms to her side, sticking her hands in her pockets. "I'm willing to risk anything if it means finding my aunt and uncle," she said softly.

Sanjay couldn't blame her. He would be willing to face even aliens if it meant getting to his mom.

He sighed. Though he still wanted to find out what had happened to the teachers, he knew it would be smarter for the three of them to stick together.

"Okay," he said. "We start with getting out of here and finding our families. Then we all can come back and help the teachers and the rest of the students."

The other two nodded.

"How are we going to get out of the school though?" Now that they'd decided on a course of action, his mind was already whirring with potential plans. "The CAPPers have this place on lockdown. It was hard enough to sneak down here—we got lucky."

Chloe tiptoed back through the main office and peeked around the door into the hallway. After a moment, she quickly gestured for them to join her.

"The main doors are just a few feet away," she whispered. "No one is around right now. What if we just . . . slip out?"

It was true. Sanjay glanced down the hallway—no sign of CAPPers coming in their direction. He didn't hear any voices or footsteps in the distance either. The school's front doors were maybe ten steps away from the main office.

He looked to Luis, who shrugged and said, "I'm in if you guys are in."

It would be risky, but they just might be able to make it unnoticed.

Sanjay nodded. "Let's do it."

After one last check to make sure no one seemed to be heading down the hall, the three of them sprinted toward the school's front entrance. Chloe pulled ahead of the boys, reaching out her arms for one of the doors.

And then Sanjay saw it.

There was a small black box wedged on the top of the door frame, and a thin wire that snaked down until it met the door's push bar.

Most importantly he noticed the small red light that was blinking, even when everything else was dead.

"Chloe, wait!" he hissed, but it was too late. Chloe turned her head when she heard Sanjay, but she had already shoved on the push bar.

A high-pitched beeping filled the air.

CHAPTER 7

They stared up at the box with wide eyes.
Apparently the CAPPers had rigged up some
kind of alarm using old electronics. Chloe
pushed at the door again, but it wouldn't budge
more than a few inches. She groaned. "It won't
open! I think they've blocked it from the
outside. I'm so sorry, guys!"

"Never mind that now," Luis hissed. "We
need to hide! Quick!"

There was nothing in the front entrance
that could hide them, so they raced back into
the main office. Sanjay dove under the couch
in the waiting area. He just fit if he stretched
out on his stomach, and it was low enough
that he hoped no one would be able to see him

unless they bent down to check underneath. From his vantage point, he saw Chloe scramble under the secretary's desk. He couldn't see Luis and hoped that he had found cover.

Only seconds later, they heard several pairs of quick footsteps in the hallway. After a moment, the alarm went silent.

"What set off the alarm, John?" someone asked. Sanjay recognized the voice—it was Paula, one of the other CAPPers they'd spoken with before.

"Don't know," John said. "It doesn't look like anyone is out here."

The door to the main office flung open. Sanjay couldn't see their faces from this position, but he saw that there were three CAPPers holding candles. He tried to breathe as quietly as possible, his face pressed against the carpet.

The candlelight passed through the room in slow arcs, and Sanjay worried his frantic heartbeat would be loud enough that everyone would be able to hear it.

He saw feet moving. The doors to the

teachers' lounge and the private offices opened and closed one by one as the CAPPers checked them.

"Doesn't look like anyone is in here either," Paula said.

"And you're sure that the alarm couldn't just glitch and go off on its own?" a third CAPPer asked. Sanjay froze. It was Max.

"Maybe," John said. "We were barely able to rig this thing together in the first place."

The CAPPers were quiet for a moment, and then John made a sound like he was blowing into his hands.

"We need to start thinking about how we're going to stay warm if we want to last through the winter," Max said. "You think winters are cold around here now, just wait until we're trying to keep this building warm without electric heat when the temperature dips into the negatives."

Winter? thought Sanjay in alarm. *It's only October. How long do they plan to be here?*

"We found some old metal trash cans in the basement," Paula said. "If we break down some of the desks for firewood, we could get some fires going."

Max laughed humorlessly. "That would be a great idea, except the desks in this school are all plastic and metal. I doubt there's any real wood in them."

"We could burn the books?" John suggested.

"I don't think we're *that* desperate yet. And I'd rather deal with a whole bunch of aliens than the wrath of Mr. O'Donnell if you try to burn his books."

"Well do *you* have any ideas?" Paula asked sullenly.

"There's a bunch of trees just outside the perimeter fence of the school," Max said. "We have axes, so that's where we can get firewood."

"Outside?" Paula blurted. "But what about the Visitors?"

"I'm not going out there," John said quickly. "I'm not risking my life for some stupid kids."

"Look," Max said through gritted teeth. "If those kids freeze or starve or get hurt in any way, then they're useless to us and our plan, got it? And besides, if the aliens have an attack force on the ground, you can bet that they're currently focused on the major cities and military bases. They're not going to be wasting the early days of their attack lurking in the woods behind a suburban high school."

"Fine," Paula said. Sanjay could almost *hear* her glaring at Max.

"I'm gonna do a head count on the kids in the library," Max said, "and make sure everyone's all right."

Sanjay heard Max leave the room. But that still left the two other CAPPers standing near the door to the hallway.

"Be careful if you go down to the basement," Paula said. "While I was down there looking for supplies, she nearly escaped."

"Which one?" John asked.

"Who do you think?" Paula said sarcastically.

John didn't laugh. "I told you she was tough. Don't underestimate her."

"Why do we even have to spend time and resources keeping her down there?"

"Because," John said coldly, "if she escapes—if she's able to make contact—then our whole plan is ruined."

Sanjay watched the two CAPPers leave the main office, pulling the door shut behind them. He waited another minute before allowing himself to breathe freely again. He rolled out from under the couch as Chloe crawled out from under the desk.

She peered around the corner of the desk toward the hallway.

"That was *way* too close," she whispered before straightening.

Sanjay brushed the dust off his jeans. "Where's Luis?"

The door to the teachers' lounge opened slowly. Sanjay felt his heart make a panicked leap before he realized it was just Luis.

"Didn't they check the teachers' lounge?" Sanjay asked.

"Not right away," Luis said. "I had time to hide in the supply closet. Luckily they didn't check that closely."

"We got lucky," Sanjay said. "Now, let's get

back to the library before it's too late. If they've already started the head count of students, we're in big trouble."

"We can't go back yet," Chloe said. "Now that the alarm's gone off, they'll be even more on their guard. It won't be as easy to sneak out of the library a second time."

"Besides, now we know for sure that the teachers and Officer Mendoza are locked up in the basement."

Sanjay's heart sank. "Yeah—who do you think they're so worried about her contacting?"

"The aliens?" Chloe said.

Luis snorted. "Why would she do that?"

She shrugged. "It happens in movies all the time. There are always some people who decide that humans are on the losing team and try to team up with the aliens."

"Officer Mendoza would never do that," Luis said. "I could totally see her leading a resistance force against the aliens. She would be one of the last ones fighting."

"*We* know that," Chloe said. "But maybe *they* don't."

Sanjay shook his head. "That's not it. Why don't you just come out and say it? I was wrong about Max. Officer Mendoza was right to be suspicious of CAPP, and now they've got her locked in the basement because they know that if she escapes, she'll expose them. This is all my fault."

Chloe sighed. "It's all right, Sanjay. I wanted to trust Max too."

"She could have been trying to contact the emergency shelter," Luis said.

Sanjay nodded grimly. "Yeah, I bet she was trying to find our families before CAPP caught her."

"We need to get down to the basement."

"I thought we agreed to just get out of here!" Chloe protested.

Sanjay clenched his jaw, his mind made up. "We already tried that. The CAPPers have probably rigged all the outside doors with alarms and barricades. Freeing the adults is our best chance of getting out of here."

They checked to see that the hallway was clear and then hurried toward the stairwell.

A moment later they turned the corner and ran right into half a dozen armed CAPPers.

"Hi, guys," Max said. "What a coincidence," he gestured at the others standing behind him, "we were just talking about you."

CHAPTER 8

When Sanjay had decided to go to the
basement, this wasn't what he'd had in mind.
The CAPPers patted down their coat pockets
and then herded them downstairs. Without
buzzing fluorescent lights or windows, the
darkness in the basement was inky black.
Sanjay's mind raced desperately, wondering
what the CAPPers were going to do now.

If he and his friends were right about what
they had heard, the CAPPers had the teachers
and Officer Mendoza down here too. As far as
Sanjay could tell, he and his friends had been
the only ones to notice Officer Mendoza's
absence and to worry about her. Would anyone
notice if *they* were missing? And even if they

did, Max would probably just reassure them with the same sorts of lies he had been telling all along.

Sanjay kept coming back to the same question. *Why?* How did the students and faculty fit into CAPP's survival plan? What benefit were a bunch of high schoolers during an alien invasion?

The basement was smaller than Sanjay had thought it would be—only an open square space with two doors and walls made of unpainted cinder blocks. A couple of days ago, this area would have been humming with electricity and the whirring of machinery. Now, it was oppressively quiet, as well as damp and cold.

Max walked ahead of them, head down as though he refused to meet their eyes. Sanjay felt his face flush with anger. The least Max could do was acknowledge that he had betrayed them.

They stopped in front of a door marked **STORAGE**. Directly across from it was another door marked **BOILER ROOM**.

One of the CAPPers unlocked the storage door and shoved Sanjay, Chloe, and Luis inside.

The room was dark and filled with looming shadowy shapes, which Sanjay realized were extra desks, chairs, folding tables, and other school furniture. Some of them were piled nearly as high at the ceiling.

Max followed them in, silhouetted against the candlelight in the hallway. He leaned on a desk near the door. "You'll be safer down here. We can't have you running around the school unsupervised; it's too dangerous."

"Dangerous for us, or for you?" Chloe snapped.

Max's face was grim. "I'm here to protect you."

"You can cut the act," said Sanjay coldly. "We know you've locked up Officer Mendoza and the teachers because they weren't on board with you being in charge here."

Max shook his head. "If you'd all just trusted me, things wouldn't have gotten out of control like this." With that, Max turned around and left the room, closing the door behind him. They heard the key turn in the lock, and then it was quiet.

It was absolutely dark in the room. Sanjay heard the clatter of a desk followed by Luis complaining about his bruised shins.

And then he heard a sound that gave him hope: the whirring of a hand-crank flashlight.

As the light blossomed, Sanjay and Luis turned with amazement to look at Chloe.

She gave a modest little shrug. "They searched our coat pockets, but they didn't think to check my sweatshirt."

"I could *totally* see you leading the rebellion against the Visitors," Sanjay said.

Chloe shrugged again. "At least we can see now, but we're still trapped."

"Actually," said Luis, taking the screwdriver out of his boot, "I think I can get us out."

CHAPTER 9

Luis grabbed the flashlight from Chloe and walked over to the door. "Look at these hinges," he said, shining the flashlight on them. "They're secured flat against the wall with *screws*."

The screws were wedged in tight, but Luis was eventually able to undo all of them. The last screw fell to the floor with a *ting-ting*. Sanjay's breath caught in his throat as he half expected the door to topple over, but nothing happened. It was loose on the hinge side, but the door's lock kept it attached to the doorframe.

"Here, give me a hand!" Luis said, grabbing the tiny bit of the door's edge that was exposed.

"If we can yank on the hinge side, we should be able to twist it free."

Chloe helped Luis pull the top corner of the door toward them. As soon as there was a gap, Sanjay stuck a discarded desk leg into the crack and used it as a lever.

With a loud creaking noise of splintered wood and bent metal, the gap in the door widened and the door twisted in its frame until they were able to lift it up and out and set it against a wall. They had made more noise than they'd wanted, but Sanjay hoped it would be hard to hear from the floor above.

Chloe cranked the emergency flashlight a few more times to make sure it had enough charge, and then they stepped out into the hallway. It was still dark, but it was nice to be out of the cluttered storage room.

Chloe and Luis headed for the stairs out of the basement, but Sanjay paused when he heard a strange sound. "Wait, did you guys hear that?"

Usually he would have chalked it up to noise from machinery or a generator, but with those out of order, the noise seemed out of place—almost like . . . voices.

"I think it's the teachers!" he whispered to Chloe and Luis.

Sanjay cupped his hands against the boiler room door. "Officer Mendoza?"

There was a pause, and then a muffled voice came through from the other side of the door. "Sanjay?" Officer Mendoza asked then. "Is that you?"

"Yeah! Chloe and Luis are here with me too."

"They've got us locked in here," Officer Mendoza shouted. "All the faculty."

"Even Mr. O'Donnell?" Sanjay asked.

"Yes, he's here too," she said. "He's been down here with the others the whole time."

"Max and the other CAPPers caught us, but we're getting out of here," Chloe shouted. She turned to Sanjay and hissed, "Or at least we will if we don't get caught again before we even get out of this basement."

"We can't just leave them!" Sanjay said quietly.

Chloe shook her head vigorously. "We already decided—once we escape the school, we can find our families and *then* come back to rescue everyone. We don't have a key for this door anyway, and the hinges are on the inside so we can't use the screwdriver again."

Sanjay was torn. He didn't want to leave anyone trapped in this dark, cold basement, especially the person who had warned them about CAPP in the first place. But how were they supposed to get anyone out?

Then they heard a rumble of footsteps coming from upstairs, as if someone were running around. Doors slammed in the distance.

The three of them looked around in a panic. Sanjay's eyes took in the storage room they had just broken out of, the locked boiler room, and the stairs up to the main floor. There was only one way they could get out of the basement. But if CAPPers came pouring down those stairs any second—and it sounded like they might—then Sanjay and his friends would be right back where they started.

Sanjay looked up at the ceiling and got an idea. "In here!" he said, pulling Chloe and Luis back into the storage room. He ran over to a particularly tall pile of desks against one wall. He doubted the pile was very stable, but there was no other way for this to work.

"Here, steady the desks while I climb up," Sanjay said.

"What good will that do?" Chloe asked, even as she grabbed a desk leg to attempt to stabilize the pile.

Sanjay scrambled up and pushed on a square ceiling panel, ignoring the dust and plaster that fell in his face. "There's a crawl space up here, between these panels and the real ceiling."

"There's no way those panels will support us," Luis said.

"True, but the panels are held up by these." Sanjay pointed to one of the thin metal support beams that formed a checkerboard grid on the ceiling. "We'll just have to rest most of our weight on the beams." He pushed off the desk gently and pulled himself up into the cramped crawl space, lying flat and trying to distribute his weight as much as possible.

"We'll spread out," he called back down to his friends. "Once you're in a good spot, just lie still and try not to make any noise. With any luck, the CAPPers will search the basement, think we escaped, and leave to look for us somewhere else."

The crawl space between the panels and the actual basement ceiling was full of layers of grime and dust and crisscrossed with pipes and wires. Sanjay could hear the noises from the floor above—scuffling feet and yelling—more clearly now, but he could barely see anything. There was no way of knowing what obstacles lay in his path.

"Chloe," he called down, "hand me the flashlight. I'll crawl ahead a bit to give you some room, and then you come up next."

He heard Chloe crawl up the shaky pile of desks. The flashlight appeared through the hole in the ceiling. Sanjay grabbed it and cranked it to charge it.

Chloe pulled herself up into the crawl

space, as Luis gave her a boost. She lay down flat and edged carefully to a spot a couple of feet away from Sanjay.

Luis was halfway up the pile of desks when they heard the door to the basement stairs open. Sanjay grabbed Luis's hand and pulled as Luis kicked off the pile of desks to clamber up. He winced as the pile collapsed and the desks clattered to the floor beneath him. Once Luis was safely positioned, Sanjay slid the panel back into place so that it covered the hole in the ceiling again. The CAPPers would have heard the desks fall over, but they would find the storage room empty. Hopefully they wouldn't think to check in the ceiling.

They held still as they heard people moving around in the basement and in the room below. There were raised voices outside the storage room, but the sound was muffled and Sanjay couldn't make out what was being said.

"I bet we can get the teachers out of the boiler room through the ceiling," Luis whispered. He and Chloe began to crawl in the general direction of the boiler room.

Sanjay moved toward the storage room. "You guys do that. I'm gonna see if I can make out what they're saying."

Chloe bit her lip, looking worried, but she nodded. She placed the flashlight on one of the ceiling panels so that it shone off into the crawlspace and illuminated the way for each of them.

"Be careful," Luis whispered to him.

"You too."

Sanjay slowly, carefully repositioned himself so he could army crawl along the ceiling in direction of the shouting. He wasn't sure how secure the support grid was, and he hardly dared to breathe. With his chest pressed against the ceiling panels below him, he could feel his heart pounding. His arm scraped by a metal pipe that tore through his jacket and bit into his skin. He gritted his teeth against the pain and kept crawling. If he could just hear what the CAPPers were saying, then maybe they could get one step ahead of them.

By now Sanjay could hear the voices much more clearly, coming from below him. Sweat stung his eyes, but he willed himself to focus.

That was when he heard the creaking of the ceiling's support grid.

"No, no, no, no!" Sanjay muttered desperately under his breath. He could feel the ceiling bending underneath him.

And then with a crash, he was falling. He yelped as he hurtled to the ground below, surrounded by a shower of dust and debris and ceiling tiles. He hit the basement floor with a *whump* that knocked the breath out of him.

Sanjay lay there for a moment in a daze, trying to get his breath back, trying to get his bearings. His ears were ringing from the impact, but he could hear surprised voices all around him.

When he was finally able to look up, Sanjay saw all of the CAPPers standing around him. He quickly shoved himself onto his feet and stood up, backing away. Bits of debris dropped from his body and a cloud of dust puffed as his back hit the wall behind him. He could see the stairs to get out were all the way on the other side of the basement, blocked by about thirty armed CAPPers.

"Sanjay," Max said, shaking his head. "I'm disappointed. Why couldn't you just stay put and let us protect you?"

Sanjay straightened. "You're not protecting us—you've *kidnapped* us."

Max took a step toward him and Sanjay raised his hands in front of himself on instinct. "Whoa now," Max said. "Let's just calm down. Everything's all right. Let's just talk."

"How about you let us go? That'll show me everything's all right."

Max took another step forward, and Sanjay felt his heart speed up. His eyes darted around the room, desperate for anything he could use to fend them off if he had to.

Then the sound of feet came pounding down the stairs. "Get away from my son!" a voice snapped.

Everyone turned, and Sanjay was shocked to see his mother rush into the basement with about a dozen other parents and a handful of uniformed police officers. He'd never seen such an intensity on his mom's face before.

Max turned and gave her a smile but didn't step away from Sanjay. "Now, ma'am," he said, "we don't want any trouble here. It would be a shame if anyone got hurt."

"That's right," came Officer Mendoza's voice as she rounded the corner, followed by Chloe and Luis and the rest of the faculty members from the boiler room.

As they filed into the space, Officer Mendoza added, "So I suggest you think carefully before you do anything you'll regret, Max."

Several of the CAPPers shifted nervously, glancing from the cluster of angry parents to the group of newly freed teachers.

It was clear that the CAPPers were outnumbered.

CHAPTER 10

Sanjay's mom glared at Max. "How could you do this to our children?" she shouted, gesturing at Sanjay. This was the angriest he had ever seen his mom.

"Mom—" Sanjay tried to get her attention, but his throat felt dry.

"Not only were we dealing with an alien attack, but then we find out you've been keeping our children hostage in their own school? What were you thinking?"

"Mom!" Sanjay practically shouted this time, and everyone fell silent. "What's going on? How did all of you get here?"

Sanjay's mom turned to look at him, her brow creased with concern. "When we got to the emergency shelter, we'd all assumed the school would have transported you kids there, like the others schools did." She glared at Max again. "And then a few of these CAPP people showed up, saying they'd taken over the high school and wouldn't release anyone until everyone at the shelter agreed to stay in town and band together against the aliens."

Sanjay stared at Max in disbelief. "That was your big plan? Keep the high schoolers hostage in order to get people to cooperate?"

Max wouldn't meet his eyes.

"We weren't about to leave you kids to this so-called community group," Luis's father continued. He gestured to the police officers who'd showed up with the parents. "These officers were kind enough to help us come back for you."

"You have our full support," Officer Mendoza told him. "I'm only sorry that we lost control of this situation."

Chloe's aunt turned to Officer Mendoza and the teachers. "How did you get out? I thought they had you all locked up."

She grinned and pointed her thumb at Chloe and Luis. "These two tricksters snuck into the boiler room through the ceiling and helped us break through the door." Chloe and Luis grinned, and Luis proudly held up his screwdriver.

"You don't have to worry anymore," Officer Mendoza said then. "We're taking control over the school and will help transport everyone back to the emergency shelter. You kids are safe now, I promise."

But that didn't do much to calm Sanjay. The CAPPers had promised them the same thing. At this point, he found the words hard to take seriously even when they came from a police officer.

"The rest of the rescue party is upstairs with the students in the library and gym," Sanjay's mom said, "but when we didn't see any CAPPers upstairs we knew they must be up to something somewhere else." She looked at Max like she wanted to start yelling again.

Max opened his mouth to speak, but Sanjay cut in. "Mom, it's okay, they didn't hurt us.

I mean, yeah, they did kinda kidnap us and keep us from leaving—"

"And they were rude and threatening—" Luis chimed in.

"But," Sanjay continued, "they never actually did anything to hurt us."

Max looked mortified. "I can't excuse what happened, but I can try to explain," he said, looking at the others. "The instant the Visitors' ships appeared in the sky, CAPP mobilized. We have plans for any sort of emergency, even EMP blasts. We knew that people's first instinct would be to flee, to take their kids and get out of the town. And we knew that if everyone did that, there would hardly be anyone left in the community to help us defend against the aliens."

He took a deep breath before continuing. "So we decided to enforce a lockdown at the high school. We figured the students would be safest here anyway, and if we had the kids, then we could ensure cooperation from their families."

Sanjay's mom glared at him. "That is horrible. That is just . . . *vile*."

Max winced. "Our intentions were in the right place."

"You didn't have to steal our kids just to get us to stay and help the community," Chloe's uncle said.

"We would never abandon this town at a time like this," Luis's mom said.

"But of course we're going to do whatever it takes to get our kids back," Chloe's aunt said.

Luis's dad nodded in agreement, then looked to Officer Mendoza. "What are we going to do with the CAPPers now?" he asked. "Shouldn't they be held responsible for what they did?

All the others turned to look at Officer Mendoza, and she sighed as she considered the question. "Normally, sure, they would have to answer for what they did. But we're missing the big picture here. Aliens have attacked Earth. Things will never be normal again. Fear can make people do stupid things—"

"Really, incredibly stupid things," Ms. Kim muttered, giving Max a pointed look.

Officer Mendoza continued. "What the

CAPPers did was wrong, but they did it for the right reasons. And I'm sure they'll all find ways to make it up to us in the weeks to come. To start, CAPP can bring all of the supplies it has stockpiled to the emergency shelter to share with everyone there. The important thing now is to come together as a community and figure out how we're going to move forward from here."

Sanjay noticed tears in several eyes and jaws set in determination.

He looked at Max. He wasn't sure he'd ever be able to trust him again, but maybe he could find it in himself to forgive him. Officer Mendoza was right. They would all need each other if they hoped to survive in this new, Visitor-infested world.

Then he looked at Chloe and Luis. "So who's ready to plan a rebellion against some aliens?"

ATTACK ON EARTH

WHEN ALIENS INVADE, ALL YOU CAN DO IS SURVIVE.

DESERTED

THE FALLOUT

THE FIELD TRIP

GETTING HOME

LOCKDOWN

TAKE SHELTER

CHECK OUT ALL THE TITLES IN THE
ATTACK ON EARTH SERIES

LEVEL UP

WHAT WOULD YOU DO IF YOU WOKE UP IN A VIDEO GAME?

ALIEN INVASION — ISRAEL KEATS

LABYRINTH — ISRAEL KEATS

POD RACER — R.T. MARTIN

REALM OF MYSTICS — RAELYN DRAKE

SAFE ZONE — R.T. MARTIN

THE ZEPHYR CONSPIRACY — ISRAEL KEATS

CHECK OUT ALL THE TITLES IN THE

LEVEL UP SERIES

ABOUT THE AUTHOR

Raelyn Drake lives in Minneapolis, Minnesota, with her husband (who would help her lead the resistance against the aliens) and her rescue corgi mix, Sheriff (whom the aliens would bribe with belly rubs and tennis balls).